To Pedrín

Original title: *No*
Copyright © 2009 by Claudia Rueda
Copyright © 2009 by Editorial Océano S.L., Barcelona (Spain)
English translation copyright © 2010 by Elisa Amado
First published in Spanish by Editorial Océano S.L., Barcelona (Spain)
Published in English in Canada and the USA in 2010 by Groundwood Books
Third printing 2011

Groundwood Books / House of Anansi Press
110 Spadina Avenue, Suite 801, Toronto, Ontario M5V 2K4
or c/o Publishers Group West
1700 Fourth Street, Berkeley, CA 94710

We acknowledge for their financial support of our publishing program the
Canada Council for the Arts, the Government of Canada through the Canada
Book Fund (CBF) and the Ontario Arts Council.

Canada Council
for the Arts

Conseil des Arts
du Canada

ONTARIO ARTS COUNCIL
CONSEIL DES ARTS DE L'ONTARIO

Library and Archives Canada Cataloguing in Publication
Rueda, Claudia
No / Claudia Rueda ; Elisa Amado, translator.
Translated from the Spanish book with same title.
ISBN 978-0-88899-991-7
I. Amado, Elisa II. Title.
PZ7.R83No 2010   j863'.7   C2010-900619-4

Design by Francisco Ibarra Meza
Printed and bound in China

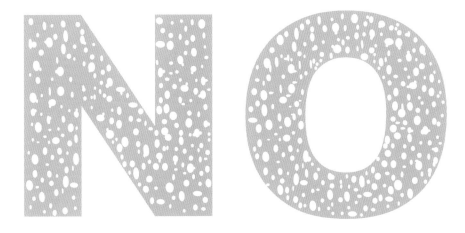

Claudia Rueda

Translated by Elisa Amado

GROUNDWOOD BOOKS / HOUSE OF ANANSI PRESS
Toronto Berkeley

"It's time to go to sleep," said mother bear.

"No," said little bear.
"I don't want to go to sleep."

"You'll freeze out here," said mother bear.

"I'm not cold,"
said little bear.

"There's no food to eat,"
said mother bear.

"I saved some berries,"
said little bear.

"Winter is very long,"
said mother bear.

"I don't mind
if it's long,"
said little bear.

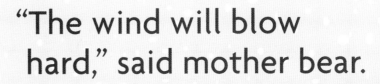

"The wind will blow
hard," said mother bear.

"I am very strong," said little bear.

"The snow will be deep,"
said mother bear.

"I love the snow,"
said little bear.

"Here comes a storm," said mother bear.

"That will be fun," said little bear.

"Mamma?"

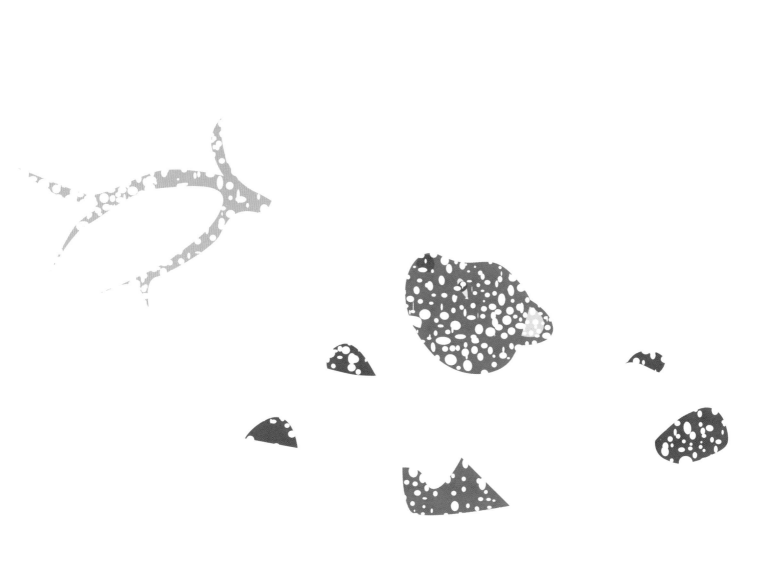

"Mamma!!"

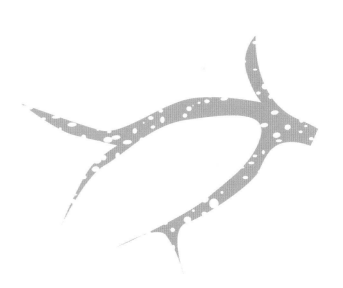

"Mamma, I'm back," said little bear.
"Winter is very long and you might get lonely."